Introduction

Supergirl Shaya is here to teach other beautiful black supergirls about black hair. In this book, you'll learn all about the science, culture, and history of black hair. But that's not all! Supergirl wants to help you love your beautiful black hair. You'll learn all the things that make your hair special and why you should love your supergirl hair. If you have ever felt bad or confused about your beautiful black girl hair, never fear! Supergirl Shaya is here!

My Hair is Lovely

10 Reasons Why My Hair is Special, Beautiful, and Powerful

We have Good Hair

Super Girl

Shem Diana Moses

Copyright © 2021 - All rights reserved.

The content contained within this book may not be reproduced, duplicated, or transmitted without direct written permission from the author or the publisher.

Under no circumstances will any blame or legal responsibility be held against the publisher, or author, for any damages, reparation, or monetary loss due to the information contained within this book, either directly or indirectly.

Legal Notice:

This book is copyright protected. It is only for personal use. You cannot amend, distribute, sell, use, quote or paraphrase any part, or the content within this book, without the consent of the author or publisher.

Disclaimer Notice:

Please note the information contained within this document is for educational and entertainment purposes only. All effort has been executed to present accurate, up to date, reliable, complete information. No warranties of any kind are declared or implied. Readers acknowledge that the author is not engaged in the rendering of legal, financial, medical or professional advice. The content within this book has been derived from various sources. Please consult a licensed professional before attempting any techniques outlined in this book.

By reading this document, the reader agrees that under no circumstances is the author responsible for any losses, direct or indirect, that are incurred as a result of the use of the information contained within this document, including, but not limited to, errors, omissions, or inaccuracies.

Publisher: Flourishing Seeds Ltd

Table of Contents

A Message From Shaya the Supergirl 1

A Poem for Supergirls 2

Chapter 1: Our Hair is Unique 3

Chapter 2: Locs and Dreads 7

Chapter 3: Afros 11

Chapter 4: Braids 15

Chapter 5: Weaves, Wigs, and Wraps 19

Chapter 6: Caring for Supergirl Hair 23

Chapter 7: Black Hair History 27

Chapter 8: We Don't Have to Change Our Curls 31

Chapter 9: Fighting for Our Curls 35

Chapter 10: Don't Touch My Hair 39

Conclusion 43

Notes: 44

Author Biography: 47

A Message From Shaya the Supergirl

My name is Supergirl Shaya. I am a strong black girl with all kinds of superpowers that help me fight any battles that come my way.

I have something special that I carry with me wherever I go. It connects me to all the super energy that gives me my supergirl powers. Whenever I look at it, I'm reminded of how powerful, strong, beautiful, and super I am. You have that same something special too. Do you know what it is?

It's your hair!

Our hair is like an antenna. It helps us connect with other supergirls around us so we can tell them our stories and share our strengths. It shows everyone around us how super we are. Our hair soaks up the sun, rainbows, and everything magic in the world. All that magic charges us up. WHIRR! And now we're filled with supergirl energy and ready to go.

There are so many reasons why our hair is so special and I'm here to share that with you, one supergirl to another.

A Poem for Supergirls

I am a supergirl

Black and strong and proud

On my head, I wear my hair

Just like a super crown

Whether I'm in an afro-puffs

Or twist out kind of mood

Whether it's wild in the mornings

Or a fancy kind of do

No matter how I wear it

I never will forget

My hair shows off my pride, my strength

and my empowerment

I don't need to change my hair

or try to make it straight

Because I know my natural hair

Is pretty super great.

Chapter 1:
Our Hair is Unique

People from different places around the world have different kinds of hair, including black people. Black people's hair is unlike anyone else's. It's beautiful, special, and cool too!

Black people come from Africa where the sun is bright and hot. Our skin is dark because it is filled with melanin, which protects us from the sun. Just like our skin, our hair grew to protect us from the sun. Our hair grows into coily spirals to help our bodies stay cool and keep us from getting burned. It's like a magic crown of protection that we carry around everywhere we go.

When black people were stolen away from Africa, they shaved our heads to try and make us forget where we came from. They wanted us to feel bad about our culture, our brown skin, and our special hair. It's a good thing that black people are so strong because we've never forgotten the power of our hair. We come up with cool and creative ways to take care of it, style it, decorate it, and show the world how proud we are to be black. And man do we have a lot to be proud of!

Black hair is magical. Our hair can stretch, spring, and bounce. It defies gravity and reaches up towards the sky. There are many words you can use to talk about beautiful black hair:

- Afro-textured
- Kinky
- Curly
- Wooly
- Coily

However you describe it, black hair is super-duper. Every supergirl's hair is different. Some have tight curls that poof out like a cloud. Others have waves and ringlets that hang down and bounce around. No matter the texture, our hair is lovely and unique.

When I wear my natural black hair, it fills me up with pride. It reminds me of all the strong black supergirls who came before me. It connects me to my culture so I'm never alone. With my super crown of kinky hair, there's nothing I can't do.

OUR HAIR IS MAGICAL

Super Girl Shaya

Chapter 2:
Locs and Dreads

Black hair can do something no other hair can do. We twist our hair up tight, then we let it grow. It starts to form strands, like ropes. Those are called 'locs'! If you take good care of them, eventually they'll start growing like that on their own. You can even grow locs just by leaving your hair alone to do its supergirl thing. Locs that are made this way are called "freeform locs". If you tried to make straight hair into locs, it would just fall apart the first time you wash it. But not kinky, curly black hair!

Some people call them dreads, twists, or dreadlocks. I just call them beautiful! Some locs are skinny and neat. Others are big and wild. Some people's locs are short and bouncy. Others' hang down all the way to the floor.

Lots of people wear locs because they are easy to take care of. All you have to do is wash and twist them every once in a while. You can wake up, give them a shake, and BAM! You're ready to go!

Some people call locs 'dirty' but they couldn't be more wrong. They're elegant and beautiful, fit for the most important people. Locs were worn by the Pharaohs of Egypt to show off their royalty. Warriors in Kenya wore locs to show everyone how powerful they were. In Jamaica, they believe their locs make them look like lions. Just like lions, supergirls are strong, beautiful, and powerful leaders. In the Bible, Samson was given superpowers as long as he let his locs grow. Sounds perfect for a beautiful brown-skinned princess or a strong, powerful supergirl!

Lots of super special supergirls wear their hair in locs. Toni Morrison is a writer who writes books especially for black girls and she has beautiful locs. Whoopi Goldberg does lots of amazing things, all while wearing her locs. She makes movies and TV shows, and was even the first woman ever to host the Academy Awards! Supergirls with locs can do anything and everything!

Locs make me feel free and special. No one can rock a head full of locs like a supergirl. You can do anything with your locs. You can wrap them up in a bun like a classy lady. You can wear them down and flip them back and forth with sass. You can put them in a fancy updo like a pretty princess or you can throw them in a ponytail when you've got supergirl things to do. However you wear your locs, you'll look amazing, supergirl!

OUR HAIR IS BEAUTIFUL

Super Girl Shaya

Chapter 3:
Afros

An afro is what happens when you let black hair grow and grow. It doesn't take much work, time, or trips to the salon to grow a super groovy afro, just a little patience while you let it grow. Afros are round and beautiful, like a dandelion puff. They bounce and shake and make a halo around our heads. Afros make us look like angels (even when we don't act so angelic). I think it's pretty super that our hair can look so beautiful even if we do nothing to it.

Some afros are big and some are small. Some are loose and curly. Others are tight and kinky. You can keep it short or let it grow all the way up towards the sky. You can tie it up in afro puffs or make an awesome mohawk. No matter how you wear your afro, it's super.

Afros are a celebration of how special black hair is. They're like a big, bright neon sign saying, "I am so proud to be black!" Afros help you fight back against people's mean words and lies without having to do anything at all.

Supergirls who fought for our rights loved to wear afros. Way back in the 1960s and 1970s, black supergirls and superboys wore their big, beautiful afros while they marched with signs and cried out, "Black is beautiful!" One of the most famous afros ever was worn by Angela Davis, a supergirl who fought hard for the rights of black people and keeps on fighting to this day. She wore her big, beautiful afro when she marched and gave speeches. She wasn't afraid of anything, because she knew she was a supergirl.

Afros aren't just powerful. They're girly and glamorous. Diana Ross was a musical diva and one of the most beautiful women in the world. She wore her afro in tons of different shapes and styles. Actresses like Logan Browning and Uzo Aduba wore their afros along with their fancy gowns on the red carpet.

I love to wear my supergirl hair in a big, beautiful afro. It's perfect for a supergirl who's got a lot of superheroing to do. If I oversleep and I'm in a rush, there's no reason to fret. I don't need to spend a long time on my hair because it practically does itself. I shape it with an afro-pick or a comb, give it a little shake, and VOILÀ! I look like a super groovy supergirl and I'm ready to face my day.

Wearing your afro shows the whole world who you are: One of an awesome army of beautiful black supergirls all over the world.

OUR HAIR IS OUR CROWN

Super Girl Shaya

Chapter 4: Braids

When it's picture day or we have a fancy event to go to, I sit between my mama's legs so she can do my hair. She tugs, combs, and pulls and I take it like a champ (I only cry a tear or two). It's not fun to get my braids done. It feels like it takes a million years, but I use my supergirl strength and I power through. Once it's all over and I look in the mirror, I always forget my aching scalp because I look so good!

Black people have invented so many types of special braids that I can't even count them all. There are big chunky box braids that hang down to your waist. There are cornrows that wrap up to buns, ponytails, and beautiful Bantu knots. You can accessorize with beads, bobbles, clips, barrettes, and bows. Braids show us just how smart, creative, and talented black supergirls can be. Black braids are a beautiful work of art, that we get to carry around on our heads to make us even more beautiful.

But braids aren't just beautiful! They're super too. Braids help protect our hair. While our hair is in braids, it's safe from all the elements and it's not being tugged, pulled, and rustled around every day. While our hair is safe in braids, it can continue to grow safe and healthy.

In Africa, they use braids to tell a person's story. Different tribes have their own unique styles of braiding that they don't do anywhere else. They have braids that tell people where you're from, if you're married, how old you are, what you do, and who you are. Some people used their braids to send messages to God. They believe their hair connects them to the spirits and gives them power, and since I'm such a powerful supergirl, I think I agree!

During slavery, black people used braids to help survive and hold on to their culture. Slaves did not have much, but they still managed to use what they had to braid their hair. They used combs made for sheep and cleaned their hair with kerosene or cornmeal. Braids were the easiest way for slaves to protect their hair, make themselves feel beautiful, and keep them connected to their culture and homeland.

When children were being pulled away from their parents, their mothers would put rice into their hair and braid it closed. That way, their children would have food on their long journeys. Some slaves even used braids to form maps that pointed to freedom. That way they could keep their plans secret from their master's and always keep their map with them.

Braids are one way black people pass down our culture. We tell our stories and laugh with our friends while getting our hair braided at the salon. Superwomen teach supergirls how to braid so we can continue to share our culture.

When your superwoman mama was just a supergirl, she sat between her mama's legs just like you. She winced and moaned while your grandma pulled, tugged, and combed. One day when you grow up and you're a superwoman, you'll learn how to braid too. You'll braid your own supergirl's hair and make her head a work of art, just like your mama, her mama, her mama, and on and on and on.

OUR HAIR IS SPECIAL

Super Girl Shaya

Chapter 5:
Weaves, Wigs, and Wraps

There was a time when black people weren't allowed to wear their natural hair. They had to make their hair look straight so that they could work and go to school and walk around without hearing mean words. It was a very hard time for black people, but that didn't stop the creativity of black supergirls! They still wanted to feel beautiful so they invented brand new ways to accessorize their hair.

One way we make our hair look straight without gross, stinky chemicals is with weaves. People have been using weaves for years and years. They even used them back in ancient Egypt. The way we make weaves today was invented by a supergirl named Christina Jenkins back in the 1950s. She took strips of straight hair and put them into black girls' hair. Just like that, POOF! The hair underneath disappears. Stylists can glue, sew, clip, or braid the hair in place. Weaves can be long or short, black, or pink.

Some supergirls choose to wear wigs to accessorize. Actresses and performers use wigs as part of their fancy costumes. Others wear wigs because they are easy and don't take a lot of work to look good. Wigs can come in every style, color, and texture you could possibly imagine. Some wigs can stay on for days at a time. Others you can throw on and off like a hat made of hair.

Supergirls also used hair wraps. They used beautiful fabrics to cover their hair. They wrapped them in lots of unique ways. Some wraps sit on your head like a swirly cinnamon bun. Some headwraps have bows, balls, or buns. There's a million ways you can wear a headwrap!

Supergirls created all these ways to cover their hair. No matter how mean the world was, they wouldn't stop expressing themselves. I think that's super cool, but we supergirls today don't have to cover our hair if we don't want to. The powerful black women who came before us fought really hard to make the world a better place where black girls could wear their natural hair with pride.

We don't have to hide our natural hair anymore! We can wear our kinky curls with pride!

OUR HAIR IS POWERFUL

Super Girl Shaya

Chapter 6:
Caring for Supergirl Hair

Black hair is super special. It's precious like silk, gold, or fine china. But, just like any precious, valuable thing, our hair is very delicate. We have to be very careful when we take care of our hair, so that it grows healthy and strong. After all, our supergirl hair gives us our supergirl powers! If we want to be ready to fight all of our battles, we have to take care of it. Luckily, supergirl scientists have worked super hard to learn all about how our hair works. They do research and use microscopes to create the best tools to keep supergirl hair healthy!

Black hair is special and only needs to be washed once a week. Scrub your scalp until you've got an afro of bubbles to get out all the gunk and grime. Your hair will come out shiny clean and it'll even grow faster! Now it's time to get the tangles out.

Trying to get your tangles out while your hair is dry can hurt your hair. Get out all your tangles while your hair is still wet and don't forget to use a super comb made just for supergirl hair. It can be frustrating, but make sure to be patient and pull out all your tangles slowly so you don't rip any hair out. It's a good thing you have supergirl patience.

Just like you rub lotion on your skin, you have to moisturize your hair. Supergirl hair is fragile and gets dry very easily, so we have to be careful to keep it moist. There are lots of creams, oils, and sprays that are like lotion especially made for your hair. There are products for kinky and loose curls, afros, locs, and braids. Whatever kind of supergirl hair you have, there's a special product just for you and they all smell delicious! (But remember, you can't eat them.)

Sometimes we go to sleep with our hair perfect and free, and wake up with a head full of tangles. But never fear, supergirl is here with a solution. Wrap your hair with a scarf or bonnet, like a suit of armor to protect against tangles. You can even braid your hair up before you sleep, to make sure it's extra super safe and protected.

Our hair is just one part of our body. When we take care of our body, we take care of our hair. I make sure to drink plenty of water and always eat my vegetables. Even if they're yucky, I know it'll help my hair stay strong and shiny.

There are lots of things that can hurt your hair. Chemicals and flat irons make your hair straight, but they can also burn your scalp or make your hair fall out. The more you let your hair do its own special thing, the healthier it will be.

There's one last thing you can do, supergirl, to keep your hair healthy. It's the most important step of all: Show your hair love. When you love your hair, it's like a magic healing beam. ZAM! Your hair is as beautiful as can be! Tell yourself how beautiful your crown is every day. Strike a pose and flip your curls, let your pride shine through every curl.

OUR HAIR IS PERFECT

Super Girl Shaya

Chapter 7:
Black Hair History

Lots of supergirls of the past fought super hard so that we could wear our hair the way we want. There are too many to count but I want to tell you about two of them.

Let me tell you about this amazing supergirl named Madame C. J. Walker.

She was born in 1867 and had a very hard life. Her parents were both slaves and she was the very first person in her family to be born free. She had to work very hard to provide for her family and when she wasn't working, she went to school.

Madame C. J. Walker started to have problems with her hair. She had dandruff and her hair even started to fall out. This happened to a lot of black girls back then, because the products they had to use for their hair weren't good at all. However, Madame C. J. Walker didn't let that get her down. She started to make all sorts of products to help her hair. She made shampoos, creams, and oils—all sorts of things. However, she didn't keep her creations to herself. She perfected her formulas and started selling them to other black women who struggled to find ways to take care of their hair. She called her products "Madame Walker's Wonderful Hair Grower".

Madame C. J. Walker didn't stop there! She opened up a beauty school to help educate other black supergirls and help them make money. At the time, it was really hard for black women to get jobs, so Madame C. J. Walker's help made a huge difference. She gave jobs to over 40,000 black women! She traveled all around the South to teach black women how to use her products. She even taught them how to do her special hair care technique and how to sell her products door to door.

After that, she opened up her own factory. Madame C. J. Walker became the first woman to have a million dollars in the entire United States! She didn't keep her money to herself though, she wanted to use her money to help other black people and that is exactly what she did. She gave money to help send black people to school. She donated her money to homes that cared for old people and groups that worked to protect black people all across America, like the NAACP. She even built a mansion where all sorts of black artists would go to work and raise money for good causes.

I also know another supergirl who loved supergirl hair named Annie Turnbo Malone.

Annie was born in 1869 and was raised by her older sister. Her parents had both been slaves and Annie was very sick as a child, so sick that she couldn't graduate school. Still, she learned that she was really good at science and chemistry. Annie loved hair and would play salon with her sister. She started experimenting and made her own hair product for black girls. She worked hard selling her product door to door and even giving it away until it started to get really popular.

Annie opened up a school to teach black girls how to do hair called Poro College. Her school had all sorts of places where black people could spend time together safely, like a gym and a church. She even worked with Madame C. J. Walker for a time, and, just like Madame C. J. Walker, she became a millionaire! She also gave money to orphans and schools for black people.

We have these supergirls to thank for all the super products and salons for black girls that we have today. Every supergirl can be just as super as Madame C. J. Walker and Annie Turnbo Malone, even you!

OUR HAIR IS LOVELY

Super Girl Shaya

Chapter 8:
We Don't Have to Change Our Curls

Have you ever heard someone talk about good hair? Some people believe that hair is only good if it's straight and soft. They think that kinky hair is bad hair. Lots of supergirls have been told they don't have good hair. Those mean words hurt them and they carry that hurt around inside them. They put chemicals and relaxers in their hair or use flat irons and hot combs to make it flat. They try to hide their supergirl curls because they're afraid other people won't think they're beautiful.

Sometimes, all the hurt they carry around inside of them is too much and they explode! POP! All of the mean words they carry around escape through their mouth and get on all the supergirls around them. They say all sorts of mean things:

"Your hair is too nappy."

"You should get a relaxer."

"Your hair looks messy."

"You don't have good hair."

They try to hurt our feelings and get us to change our curls too. But I know the truth and so do you. All those words are just lies. We're beautiful just the way we are and so is our hair! Supergirl hair is perfect for any occasion. Afros look gorgeous at the ballet. Locs look classy in an office and lovely at a ball. Afro puffs are great for a basketball game and braids make a great first day of school look. Black girl hair fits every occasion. It looks beautiful on supergirls from caramel to midnight.

Supergirl hair is never out of style.

There are lying voices all around telling us that black hair isn't fancy, elegant, or feminine. The girls on TV all seem to have hair that's only a little bit curly or not curly at all. When we have somewhere fancy to go to, people tell us to straighten our hair so we look 'presentable'. Sometimes people who don't have supergirl hair get confused about black hair but instead of asking questions, they tell us that we should change.

Sometimes I hear these words and my heart starts to hurt. But I know I'm a supergirl and I've got just the superpower for that. I know just how to protect myself from these mean lies. All I have to do is hold my head up high and wear my natural hair with a great big grin. Suddenly, I'm surrounded by a shield of pride that nothing can get through. When mean words come my way, I just shoot back with the truth like a laser. PEW!

"I am a beautiful black girl and my hair is my crown!"

"All hair is beautiful, especially kinky curls!"

"My hair is good hair."

I can also fight back by teaching others the truth. I can share all the wisdom that I have stored up in my supergirl brain about what makes black hair so special. I can even share my powers with other supergirls when I see that they're feeling down. I tell them just how beautiful and special their curls are and just like that BAM! Those mean words and lies don't stand a chance.

There are lots of lies people might tell us to convince us that our hair isn't good hair. Good thing you're a supergirl and you know better! Good hair is hair that's worn with pride and a smile. Good hair is healthy hair. Good hair is long or short, thick or thin, black or brown, and blonde or blue. Good hair comes in Bantu knots, braids, afro puffs, and twists.

Good hair is your hair! Your hair is good hair!

OUR HAIR IS GORGEOUS

Super Girl Shaya

Chapter 9:
Fighting for Our Curls

In the past, black people weren't allowed to wear their hair naturally because the people in charge didn't understand it. They made rules that black people had to straighten or cover their hair so they would be allowed to go to school, work, or important events.

However, strong supergirls knew this wasn't right and they decided to fight back. They wore their natural hair with pride, no matter what people said. Their hair was like the superhero cape they wore while they fought for our rights.

During the Civil Rights Movement, lots of black people started to come together to make the world a better place. Supergirls and superboys from all over started to demand change. They wanted better schools, better homes, and less hate. They wanted black people to be accepted as they were and that included their hair. They were tired of having to change themselves to be accepted, so they decided to love who they were, loud and proud.

There were lots of people who wore their afros as a part of their fight. These strong supergirls wore their hair like a work of art. People let their hair grow into big beautiful afros, long elegant locs, and braids to show that they wouldn't be ashamed anymore. No matter what mean things people threw at them, they never gave up. They never gave up their beautiful supergirl curls and fought to give us a better future.

I know about a supergirl named Holly J. Mitchell who is fighting super hard for black hair. She is a Senator in the United States. She is part of a group called the CROWN coalition. CROWN stands for Create a Respectful and Open World for Natural Hair. Together, they help pass laws that protect supergirls so that we can wear our hair however we want, wherever we want, without being hurt or bullied.

When I appreciate my beautiful curls, I can see how far we've come. It's like a pair of super goggles that let me see into the past. I can see all the strong supergirls who fought so I could wear my hair with pride. My curls are a gift from them and I am so grateful.

But that's not it! My hair also lets me see into the future. I can see a better world for supergirls everywhere, a world where no one ever has to feel bad about their natural hair, where everyone appreciates supergirls just the way they are. As long as I remember just how super I am, I have the power to make that future real one day. My kinky hair gives me the power to keep on fighting just like the supergirls in the past, no matter what.

Our hair isn't just hair. It's who we are! It's worth fighting for and that's what supergirls do. Fight!

OUR HAIR IS PRECIOUS

Super Girl Shaya

Chapter 10:
Don't Touch My Hair

Black hair is super unique and grabs attention like a super magnet. I always turn heads when I'm wearing my fancy braids or my colorful bobbles, but sometimes that attention isn't always good.

People who don't have supergirl hair might have lots of questions. That's ok. It's good to ask questions. But sometimes their questions are rude or hurt my feelings.

"Is that really your hair?"

"Do you wash it?"

"Why is your hair so weird?"

When people ask these questions that I don't like, I can tell them so. I use my supergirl voice to tell them, "Hey! I don't like it when you talk to me like that."

Some people are so curious about my afro-textured hair that they want to touch it. Sometimes they even try to touch it without asking! They think that just because I'm little and brown, and have supergirl hair and supergirl skin, that they don't have to ask permission. But that's not fair! I'm not a pet at a petting zoo or a patch of dandelions. I'm a person. I'm a supergirl!

I don't have to let it happen. I'm the master of me! My body belongs to me and only me. Whenever people try to touch my hair without permission, I raise my voice and use my strongest power: A big, confident, supergirl, "No!" It doesn't matter who or what, when or how. It doesn't matter if they are a friend, a teacher, or a stranger on the street. Everyone has to ask before they touch me, especially my hair, and if I don't want to be touched, then I don't have to be.

Your hair belongs to you and only you. You decide what to do with it, how to wear it, and who can touch it. Don't let people treat you like a toy, supergirl! Instead, raise your supergirl voice and say, "Don't touch my hair!"

OUR HAIR IS GOOD HAIR

Super Girl Shaya

Conclusion

Now that I've taught you all about your supergirl hair, I hope you'll wear it with pride. You should since you've got so much to be proud of. You've got years and years of history packed into a beautiful, magic crown sitting on top of your head. When you love your curls, you don't just make yourself more super. You make all the supergirls around the world more powerful too.

Black girl hair is perfect anytime, anyplace. There's no occasion where black girl hair isn't beautiful. There's not one supergirl in the entire world who shouldn't wear their hair just as it grows out of their head. There are strong black doctors with locs. There are caramel-colored artists with big bouncy afros. There are dark-skinned dancers, singers, and actors with long gorgeous braids.

However, you choose to wear your hair, remember that you're still a supergirl. You're strong, beautiful, powerful, smart, and most of all, you're perfect just the way you are.

Your hair is lovely, supergirl! We have good hair!

Notes: 🦋🦋

Now that you know why your hair makes you so special, list the superpowers your hair gives you. What makes you love your supergirl hair?

This book is dedicated to my beautiful niece, Yara-Inara with love. 🫶

My prayer is that Yahweh will capture your mind, heart and spirit and make your life one beautiful, amazing adventure. Full of love, strength, confidence, and high self-esteem knowing that you can conquer and achieve all your dreams. 🙏

Author Biography:

Shem Diana Moses is a fervent children's diversity pen woman committed to artistically writing self-affirmation and confidence-boosting materials for young girls of color. Intrinsically motivated by her intense devotion to affirm and instill confidence in young brown and black girls, Shem writes intriguing content tailored to help them in stress relieving, accepting their uniqueness, freely expressing their creativity, attaining empowerment, and helping to improve how they feel and view themselves.

Shem strongly believes in writing as a highly effective medium in assisting both the children and the youth in discovering their inner voice and giving their inner confidence a chance to rise. She also works tirelessly to ensure that children and the youth maintain high self-esteem through innumerable black wellness and charitable projects.

Alongside writing for change, Shem is an enthusiast in charitable projects in Africa. She believes in creating growth and sustainable enterprises that promote overall growth in individuals and progressive thinking.

WWW.ShemDianaMoses.Com

Publisher: Flourishing Seeds Ltd

Notes

Notes

Notes

Notes

Notes

Notes

Notes

Notes

Notes

Notes

Notes

Notes

Notes

Notes

Notes

Notes

Notes

Notes

Notes

Notes

Notes

Notes

Notes

Notes

Notes

Notes

Printed in Great Britain
by Amazon